East of the Sun West of the Moon

Written by Peter Christen Asbjørnsen

Jørgen Engebretsen Moe

Retold by Jo Nelson

Illustrated by Marseta Hajdinjak

Collins

Chapter 1

A long time ago, and far away, a poor farmer lived with his family in a small, run-down cottage. He had so many children, he'd almost lost count. Each child was lovelier than the last. The problem was how to feed them all!

One afternoon, the family were crowded inside the cottage while a dark storm raged outside. Suddenly, above the roar of the wind, they heard a TAP, TAP, TAP.

The farmer opened the door to a blast of cold air … and a great white bear.

"Good evening," said the white bear, politely.

"Good evening!" replied the farmer, in surprise. He'd never spoken to a bear before.

"I believe your children need clothes, food and a bigger house," said the bear.

"We dream about it sometimes … " sighed the farmer.

"Then let your eldest daughter Rosa come with me," said the bear, "and I'll make your family's dream come true."

The farmer didn't know what to say.

"Take your time," said the bear. "I'll return next week."
He bowed and disappeared into the storm.

Rosa saw her father's pale face. "What's wrong?" she asked.

Slowly, he explained the bear's strange offer.

"I'll go with him," Rosa declared.

"But … " her father began.

"No buts," she replied firmly. "It's for the best."

Chapter 2

A week went by, and sure enough the bear returned. TAP, TAP, TAP. This time, it was Rosa who opened the door.

"Good evening," said the bear, politely. "Will you come with me?"

"I will," replied Rosa.

"Where are you going?" asked her youngest sisters.

"On an adventure," said Rosa.

The bear crouched down low and said, "Climb aboard."

Rosa clambered onto his shaggy white back, and together they set off across the crisp snow.

"Are you afraid?" asked the bear.

"No," replied Rosa.

The setting sun cast a rosy glow around them, and Rosa felt safe and warm against the bear's soft fur.

She must have fallen asleep because the next thing Rosa knew it was morning and a steep cliff towered above them.

The bear knocked twice on the side of the cliff and a door swung open. Rosa realised in amazement that the cliff was in fact the wall of a grand castle. She was now gazing into a majestic hall, gleaming with silver and gold.

"If you need anything," said the bear, "ring this." He handed her a small silver bell, then disappeared down a long corridor.

7

Rosa rang the bell because she was hungry … and found herself at a dining table laden with delicious food.

She rang the bell because she was thirsty … and a glass of sparkling drink appeared in her hand.

She rang the bell because she was tired … and she found herself in the softest bed she could imagine.

That night, Rosa fell asleep … and had a wonderful dream about a handsome prince.

Chapter 3

Time went by slowly in the grand castle. The little bell gave Rosa everything she needed and the bear was always very polite, but Rosa couldn't help feeling lonely.

Each night, the same handsome prince visited Rosa in her dreams, but when she awoke she felt even lonelier. "If only he were real … " she thought.

"What's wrong?" asked the bear one morning.

"Nothing," said Rosa quickly. She couldn't tell the bear about the prince. "It's just – I miss my family."

"Then let's visit them," said the bear.

As they crossed the snowy wilderness, the bear made Rosa promise one thing – not to talk to her mother on her own.

They reached the top of a hill and Rosa whooped with delight. She could see her brothers and sisters in the valley below, playing in the garden of a magnificent house.

"Thank you," whispered Rosa in the bear's ear, as they padded towards her family.

Later that afternoon, Rosa was clearing away the dinner plates when she heard footsteps behind her. It was her mother and they were alone.

"My darling daughter," said Rosa's mother. "I see sadness in your eyes."

"I'm fine," replied Rosa quickly.

"Is the bear kind to you?" her mother asked.

"Oh yes, it's not him," said Rosa. Then, before she could stop herself, she was telling her mother all about her dreams of the handsome prince. "In the dark, he seems so real," sighed Rosa.

"Well, maybe he is," said her mother, thoughtfully. She reached into the cupboard, took out a candle and put it in a pretty pouch. "Next time he comes, light this candle. Then you'll be able to see if he's really there or not."

12

Chapter 4

As the sun sank low in the sky, Rosa waved goodbye to her family and rode off on the great white bear.

"Did you speak with your mother alone?" asked the bear.

"Yes," said Rosa. "I'm sorry."

The bear sighed. "Don't follow her advice," he warned, "or it'll be unlucky for both of us."

The following night, Rosa dreamt about her handsome prince again. She sat up quietly in the dark. "I need to know if he's real," she said to herself.

Carefully, she lit the candle stub. Its flickering light revealed a handsome man, sleeping peacefully on a chair beside her bed. "My prince!" she whispered. Then she noticed a shaggy lump on the floor. "The bear's coat!" she gasped.

At that moment, a drop of wax fell from the candle onto the sleeping prince.

He woke with a start. "What have you done?" he cried.

"You're … the bear!" said Rosa, amazed.

The prince sighed. "My stepmother put a spell on me," he said. "I'm a bear in the day and myself only at night. She said if I hid my secret from you for a year, I'd be free. But I've failed, and now … "

"Now what?" said Rosa quickly.

"The spell will take me away and I must marry a troll princess."

"NO!" shouted Rosa. "What can I do?" she asked desperately.

"Come to the troll's castle," replied the prince. "The spell can only be broken if I see you again before the wedding."

"But where is it?" Rosa cried.

"East of the Sun and west of the Moon," came the prince's voice Then he was gone.

Chapter 5

At dawn, Rosa found herself sitting by the cliff face. There was no sign of the castle or the prince, only a glossy black horse. She climbed on the horse's back and rode for miles, through a dark forest and across a vast plain.

Eventually, she saw an old woman sitting on a rock, playing catch with a golden apple.

"Excuse me," said Rosa. "I'm looking for the castle which lies east of the Sun and west of the Moon."

"So you're the girl ... " murmured the old woman. "I don't know the way," she said, "but my neighbour might. Follow the path by the mountain. And take my apple – you'll need it."

Rosa thanked the old woman and followed the path. Eventually, she saw a second old woman sitting on a rock and holding a golden comb.

"Excuse me," said Rosa. "I'm looking for the castle which lies east of the Sun and west of the Moon."

"So you're the girl … " murmured the second woman. "I don't know the way," she said, "but my neighbour might. Follow the path along the river. And take my comb – you'll need it."

Rosa thanked the old woman and followed the path. Eventually, she saw a third old woman sitting on a rock with a golden spinning wheel.

"Excuse me," said Rosa. "I'm looking for the castle which lies east of the Sun and west of the Moon."

"So you're the girl … " murmured the third woman. "I don't know the way," she said, "but the East Wind might. Follow this path to the coast. And take my spinning wheel – you'll need it."

Chapter 6

Rosa rode for many days. Eventually, she reached the coast and met the East Wind outside his house.

"Come and rest a while," he said. "You look worn out."

Warmed by the fire and strengthened by some soup, Rosa told him where she needed to go.

"I've blown all over the world," said the East Wind, "but never east of the Sun and west of the Moon. That'll take a lot of puff."

"If it's too far … " began Rosa.

The East Wind looked at her very seriously. "Nowhere is too far for me," he declared. "We'll set off at first light."

Riding the East Wind was very different to riding a bear or a horse. Rosa wasn't sure how to climb onto his billowy back.

"You can't hurt me," he assured her. "Just hold on tight!"

Soon they were tearing across the sky, scattering clouds behind them. They flattened entire forests beneath them and whisked up massive ocean waves.

In one final gust, the East Wind
blew them to the gates of
a shadowy castle which lay east
of the Sun and west of the Moon.

"Thank you!" Rosa exclaimed,
but the East Wind didn't
hear her. He'd slumped to
the ground, totally puffed out.

23

Chapter 7

"What do I do now?" wondered Rosa. She stared at her golden apple for inspiration.

"I want that apple!" came a high-pitched voice.

Rosa looked up and saw a snooty young woman, with skin as grey as rock. "The troll princess!" she gasped.

"Give that apple to me!" cried the troll.

"Only if I can see the prince," said Rosa.

"Very well," the troll sniffed. "Come back tonight."

In exchange for the apple, Rosa was taken to a prison cell in a tall tower. There lay her prince, but he was sleeping so deeply she couldn't wake him.

The next morning, Rosa sat at the castle gates, combing her hair with the golden comb.

"I want that comb!" cried the troll princess.

"Only if I can see the prince again," said Rosa.

"Very well," the troll sniffed. "Come back tonight."

Once again, the prince was in a deep, deep sleep. Rosa cried out desperately, "Wake up, my prince. It's me – Rosa!"

Her cries couldn't wake the sleeping prince, but they were heard by the prisoner next door …

Chapter 8

Next morning, the prisoner called to the prince. "A girl called Rosa visited you last night, but you wouldn't wake up."

"Rosa!" cried the prince. "If only I could see her then I'd be free. But tomorrow I'm to be married and then it'll be too late."

The troll princess was clever and cruel. She'd been putting sleeping powder in the prince's bedtime drink so that he wouldn't wake up and see Rosa. But trolls have one weakness – gold. When the troll saw Rosa with the golden spinning wheel, she wanted it more than anything.

"Give me that wheel!" she shouted.

"Only if you let me see the prince again," said Rosa.

"Very well," the troll sniffed.
"Come back tonight."

Once again, the troll put a large dose of sleeping powder in the prince's drink. This time he knew better than to drink it. He only pretended to be asleep and, when Rosa was let into his room, he ran to greet her.

"My prince!" cried Rosa.

"My princess!" he replied.

"NO!" screamed the troll princess from the doorway. "He wasn't meant to see you! Now you've broken the spell and everything's ruined!" Her face scrunched up with rage and her body grew harder and harder. Within moments, she was nothing but a crumbling lump of rock.

As for Rosa and her prince, the East Wind blew them
back to her family's home. They were married
in the garden among the springtime flowers,
with too many bridesmaids and
pageboys to count. And, of course,
they lived happily ever after.

Rosa's adventures

Ideas for reading

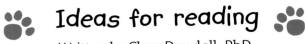

Written by Clare Dowdall, PhD
Lecturer and Primary Literacy Consultant

Reading objectives:
- increase familiarity with a wide range of books including fairy stories and retell orally
- identify themes and conventions
- ask questions to improve understanding
- draw inferences and justify these with evidence
- make predictions from details stated and applied

Spoken language objectives:
- ask relevant questions to extend their understanding and knowledge

Curriculum links: Geography – locational knowledge, geographical knowledge

Resources: compass; globe; ICT for research

Build a context for reading

- Ask children to recap their knowledge about compass points and to draw a compass.
- Look at the front cover and ask children to suggest where this traditional tale might originate. Locate the Arctic Circle on a globe and see which countries belong to this geographical area.
- Read the blurb together. Challenge children to notice anything unusual about the story.

Understand and apply reading strategies

- Read Chapter 1 together. Ask children to listen for common features that appear in traditional tales (story language, poor characters, strange magical creatures, unusual proposals and promises).

31

Ideas for reading

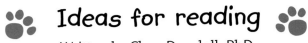

Written by Clare Dowdall, PhD
Lecturer and Primary Literacy Consultant

Reading objectives:
- increase familiarity with a wide range of books including fairy stories and retell orally
- identify themes and conventions
- ask questions to improve understanding
- draw inferences and justify these with evidence
- make predictions from details stated and applied

Spoken language objectives:
- ask relevant questions to extend their understanding and knowledge

Curriculum links: Geography – locational knowledge, geographical knowledge

Resources: compass; globe; ICT for research

Build a context for reading
- Ask children to recap their knowledge about compass points and to draw a compass.
- Look at the front cover and ask children to suggest where this traditional tale might originate. Locate the Arctic Circle on a globe and see which countries belong to this geographical area.
- Read the blurb together. Challenge children to notice anything unusual about the story.

Understand and apply reading strategies
- Read Chapter 1 together. Ask children to listen for common features that appear in traditional tales (story language, poor characters, strange magical creatures, unusual proposals and promises).